GLUEPOTBOOKS

©2019 Neil G Henderson & Scarlett Rickard

ISBN: 978-0-9957943-3-7

Written by Neil G Henderson. Illustrated by Scarlett Rickard. Published by Gluepot Books.

www.gluepotbooks.com

BILLY McGEE AND TINY McFLEA

BY NEIL G. HENDERSON · ILLUSTRATED BY SCARLETT RICKARD

Here is the tale of Billy McGee
And his strange little pet called Tiny McFlea.

Lots of kids have cats and dogs
Hamsters, rabbits and slimy frogs.

But a flea is a very unusual pet
You couldn't just take him to see the vet.

The vet would cry:

Billy would make Tiny circus tricks,
Like a trapeze and stilts from cocktail sticks

He even taught him how to juggle
With peppercorns, which was a struggle.

Then one day to the town's excitement
A circus arrived and all were invited.
CIRCUS
AMAZING
EXCITING
INCREDIBLE
IN THE PARK
THIS WEEKEND!
I must take Tiny to see the acts,
Like the lions, the clowns
and the acrobats.

The big night arrived and he raced to the show
And Billy got a seat in the very front row.

As the lights went up, to Billy's dismay
Wee Tiny McFlea had hopped away.

The strong-man raised his weights up high
As Tiny bit his muscled thigh.

His screams echoed around the place
A look of pain across his face.

He dropped the bar onto the floor
Which crashed into the clown's car door.

Coco the driver lost control
And hit the Big Top centre pole.

Lucky for him he landed safely
On Lena the circus' bearded lady.

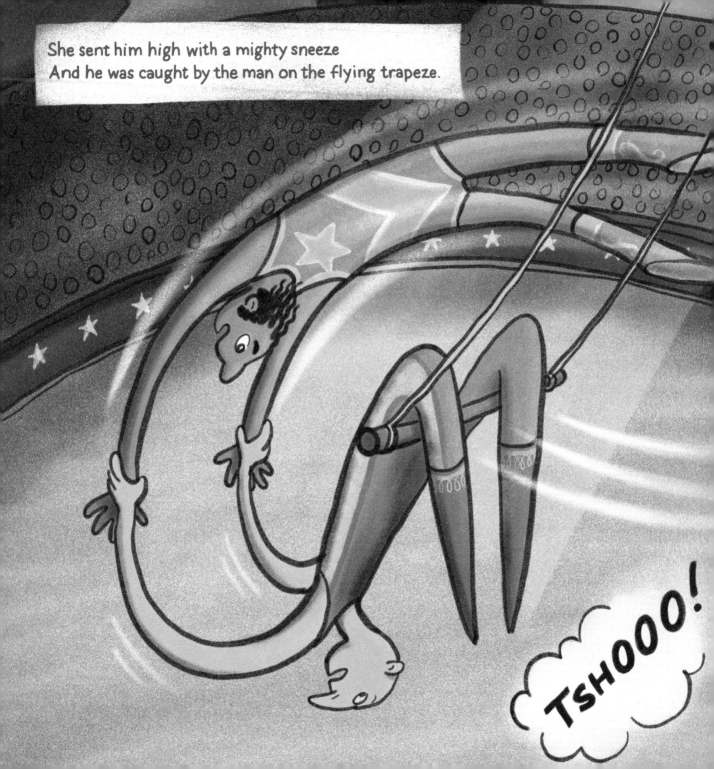

She sent him high with a mighty sneeze
And he was caught by the man on the flying trapeze.

The sneeze from Lena gave the horses a fright
And the magician's pigeons all took flight.

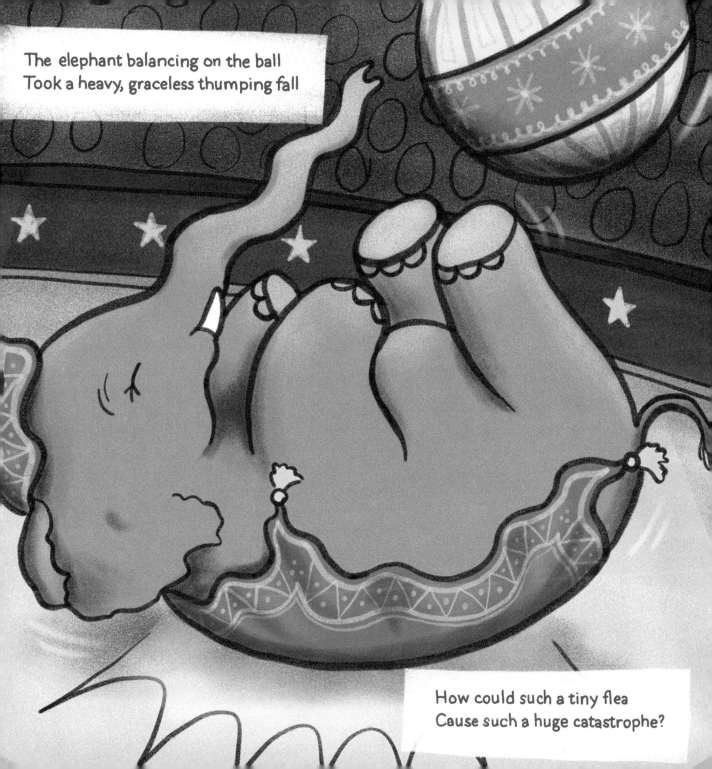

The Ringmaster's eyes filled up with tears
"I'm ruined," he said, but then came cheers.

"Bravo! Encore!" the crowd all clapped,
The Ringmaster, slightly bewildered,
doffed his hat.

CPSIA information can be obtained
at www.ICGtesting.com
Printed in the USA
BVHW021021090819
555506BV00018B/1600/P